HAPPILY EVER AFTER

Fairy Godmothers

KATE RIGGS

CREATIVE EDUCATION

Published by Creative Education
P.O. Box 227, Mankato, Minnesota 56002
Creative Education is an imprint of
The Creative Company
www.thecreativecompany.us

Design by Stephanie Blumenthal
Production by Christine Vanderbeek
Art direction by Rita Marshall
Printed in the United States of America

Photographs by Alamy (AF archive, INTERFOTO, Hilary Morgan, Moviestore Collection Ltd), Dover Publications Inc. (120 Great Fairy Paintings; Children's Book Illustrations; Imps, Elves, Fairies & Goblins), Graphic Frames (Agile Rabbit Editions), Mary Evans Picture Library (Peter & Dawn Cope Collection)

Illustrations pages 7, 20, 21 © 1983 Roberto Innocenti

Library of Congress Cataloging-in-Publication Data
Riggs, Kate.
Fairy godmothers / by Kate Riggs.
p. cm. — (Happily ever after)
Summary: A primer of the familiar fairy-tale characters of fairy godmothers, from how they use their magical powers to those they help, plus famous stories and movies in which they have appeared. Includes index.
ISBN 978-1-60818-241-1
1. Fairy tales. 2. Sponsors—Juvenile literature. I. Title.

GR550.R45 2013
398'.45—dc23   2011050868

First edition
9 8 7 6 5 4 3 2 1

TABLE OF CONTENTS

*"Once upon a time,
there was a fairy godmother.
She looked after a beautiful princess."*

Fairy godmothers are characters you can find in fairy tales. A fairy tale is a story about magical people and places.

Fairy godmothers have magical powers. Good fairy godmothers use their magic to keep people safe. They also use their magic to help others.

Some fairies are not good. They use their magic for evil. A bad fairy can cast spells called **curses**. Even a fairy godmother cannot undo a curse. But she can change the spell to make it better.

Fairy godmothers are the helpers in a fairy tale. They might act like parents to characters who are **orphans**. Fairy godmothers listen to people's problems. They give other characters advice, too.

Someone who is in trouble calls on a fairy godmother. The fairy godmother might help a princess meet a prince. Or she might help a poor girl look like a princess.

A fairy godmother waves her wand to use her magic. She can turn everyday clothes into beautiful dresses. She can turn bad fairies' curses into good spells.

There are seven fairy godmothers in the story *Sleeping Beauty*. There is also one bad fairy. The bad fairy says the princess will die. But the seventh fairy godmother changes the curse. She says that the princess will just fall asleep. A prince will wake her.

16

The fairy godmother is a very different character in the movie *Shrek 2*. She is **selfish**. She wants her son, Prince Charming, to marry a princess so that she can be more powerful.

Most fairy godmothers are good. They help people get what they want.

"The princess wanted to go to the ball. Her fairy godmother made her into the most beautiful girl at the ball. The prince danced with the princess. And they all lived happily ever after."

WRITE YOUR OWN FAIRY TALE

Copy this short story onto a sheet of paper.
Then fill in the blanks with your own words!

Once upon a time, there was a princess named _____.

She had a fairy godmother named _____. The princess

wished that she could _____. One day, she saw a _____.

She asked her fairy godmother to _____. The fairy

godmother cast a spell to _____. The princess

was _____! She married a _____ prince named

_____. They lived happily ever after.

GLOSSARY

curses—spells that make something bad happen

orphans—children who do not have parents

selfish—not thinking or caring about others

READ MORE

Matthews, Caitlin. *How to Be a Princess*. New York: Carlton Books, 2009.

Peters, Stephanie True. *A Princess Primer: A Fairy Godmother's Guide to Being a Princess*. New York: Dutton Children's Books, 2006.

WEB SITES

Cinderella and the Fairy Godmother Jigsaw Puzzle
http://www.gamesloon.com/free-puzzle-7/jigsaw-games-20/cinderella-the-fairy-godmother-jigsaw-puzzle-26478.html
Put together this puzzle to see the picture of Cinderella and her fairy godmother.

DLTK's Fairy Tales Activities: Sleeping Beauty
http://www.dltk-teach.com/rhymes/sleeping-beauty/index.htm
Find Sleeping Beauty crafts to make and pictures to color.

INDEX